Heather Hits Her First Home Run

© Copyright 1989
Text by Ted Plantos
Illustrations by Heather Collins
Design by Glyphics Inc.

Published in March 1989 by:
Black Moss Press
1939 Alsace Avenue
Windsor, Ontario
Canada N8W 1M5

with the assistance of the
Canada Council and the
Ontario Arts Council.

Black Moss Press Books are
distributed in Canada and
the United States by:

Firefly Books
250 Sparks Avenue
Willowdale, Ontario
Canada M2H 2S4

All orders should be directed
there.

ISBN 0-88753-185-7
First printing March 1989

Printed in Canada by
The National Press,
Toronto, Ontario

For Tom Stuckey and our 1981
Pee Wee Championship Team —
East Toronto Baseball Association.

Heather Hits her First Home Run

By Ted Plantos

Illustrated by
Heather Collins

Black Moss Press

There were runners on all three bases and two out when Heather came to bat. This was Heather's first year playing Tee-ball, and she hadn't had a hit yet. She wanted to give the ball a good whack.

Every time she had been to the plate, the ball flew off her bat into the air, and someone would catch it. Heather wondered why her fly balls were always caught, especially because the fielders seemed to drop just about every other fly ball.

Heather remembered her friend and teammate, Jeffrey, telling her to "sting the ball".

"But I'm not a bumblebee," she told Jeffrey.

"If you want to sting the ball, you have to put some muscle behind your swing," Jeffrey explained.

Now Jeffrey was on third base
waiting for Heather to hit
him home.

C'mon, Heather," Jeffrey shouted,
"muscle it!"

Heather blushed when her mother and some other people laughed at what Jeffrey said. Then everyone started shouting, "C'mon, Heather, muscle the ball..." Even her coach, Mr. Stuckey, got into the act. Only he said, "...a little four-bagger, Heather."

Heather was nervous. Her stomach felt funny when she stepped up to the tee.

"Some days," Heather thought, "the ball looks as big as a watermelon. But today it looks as small as a dime."

Heather lifted the bat and closed her eyes. She swung really hard, but all she heard was a whoosh. She opened her eyes and saw the ball still sitting on the tee.

When she swung the bat another four times and missed, everyone stopped shouting for her to hit a home run. But her mother still cheered on. "You can hit the ball, Heather!"

Heather felt a little tear in each of her eyes. They tickled her face when they dripped down her chin. She began to sniffle when she stepped up to the ball again.

She could hear Jeffrey calling, "Hit me in Heather."

The third baseman, a
little red-haired boy
named Stevey, was the
noisiest
player
on the other
team.

When he shouted,
"Easy out...
she's too weak to hit
the ball," Heather's face
turned red.

But this time she wasn't
blushing. She was angry.
"I'll show him," Heather
said, as she closed her
eyes and swung.

Heather heard a cracking sound and a lot of people cheering. When she opened her eyes, she saw the ball she had hit climbing higher and higher in the air.

Stevey and two other players on the other team were screaming, "I've got the ball..." when it curved in the air and started to fall.

Three baseball gloves reached for the ball, but it bounced between Stevey and his teammates and they crashed together and fell into a heap.

Heather had just passed third base and was on her way home when Stevey picked up the ball.

She could see the player at the plate waiting to catch the ball and tag her out. Heather forgot about being angry at Stevey. She even forgot about crying...

Heather was having fun.

She slid toward home plate just as the ball popped into the catcher's mitt. He slapped Heather's ankle.

The umpire, Mrs. Quinn, leaned over and shouted. "You're out!"

"All right, that's three out!" the catcher cheered as he leaped up from the cloud of dust at Heather's heels.

"Does that mean the runs don't count? Heather asked. "No, Heather," Mrs. Quinn explained, "the three runs scored before the catcher tagged you out... All three runs count for your team."

Everyone cheered when Heather ran back to the bench. Her mother was jumping up and down. And Jeffrey was screaming, "I knew you could hit the ball, Heather!"

"I'm sorry for not getting a home run, Mr. Stuckey," Heather said to her coach.

Mr. Stuckey smiled. "Heather, you just hit a four-bagger. As far as I'm concerned, it was a home run!"